This book
belongs to

This edition published by Parragon Books Ltd in 2015

Parragon Books Ltd
Chartist House
15–17 Trim Street
Bath BA1 1HA, UK
www.parragon.com

ISBN 978-1-4723-6709-9

Printed in China

Rapunzel

Bath · New York · Cologne · Melbourne · Delhi
Hong Kong · Shenzhen · Singapore · Amsterdam

Once upon a time, in a faraway land, a husband and wife were expecting a baby. One day, the wife was looking out of the window at the garden next door. She saw lettuce called 'rapunzel' growing in a patch. Suddenly she wanted some.

"My dear husband," she said, "I simply must have some of the delicious-looking lettuce from that garden."

"That garden belongs to a witch," whispered the husband. "She is said to be the most fearsome witch in all the land! But if you want some of her rapunzel, then I will get it for you."

That night, the husband climbed over the wall into
the witch's garden and picked some lettuce. But just
as he was about to leave, the witch appeared!

"M-m-madam," the husband stammered. "My wife is
expecting a baby and she craves this rapunzel lettuce."

"I will let you have some of my lettuce, which I have planted and which I have tended with such care," the witch replied, "but I want something in return. When the child is born you will give it to me."

The husband agreed, never dreaming that the witch was serious.

A few months later, a beautiful baby girl was born.

"What shall we name her?" the new mother asked as she and her husband admired their daughter.

The new father smiled down at the baby. "We shall call her Rapunzel, after the lettuce that you wanted so badly."

Suddenly, the witch appeared at the window.

"She is mine! Remember your promise," the witch
said to the father. Then the witch snatched the child
and disappeared.

Rapunzel grew to be beautiful and kind. She had long, golden hair and an enchanting voice. But she was lonely. The witch was afraid someone would take Rapunzel from her, so she locked the girl in a high tower with only sewing to keep her busy. Rapunzel could see the world through her window, but she could not leave the tower.

The only way into the tower was through the window. When the witch wanted to visit Rapunzel, she stood at the bottom of the tower and called: "Rapunzel, Rapunzel, let down your hair to me."

Rapunzel would hang her long plait out of the window and the witch would climb up. Every day and every night the witch called out to her, and every day and every night Rapunzel let down her hair. And so it was that years passed and Rapunzel only ever saw the witch.

Rapunzel was singing at her window one night when a handsome prince happened to ride by. The prince heard Rapunzel's beautiful voice and saw her at the window of the tower.

As he continued on his way, the prince couldn't stop thinking about the lovely young woman in the window. He began to ride by the tower every evening to catch a glimpse of her.

One night, the prince heard the witch call to Rapunzel.
He watched in amazement as the old woman climbed up
Rapunzel's hair.

The prince visited the tower for the next three nights. Each time he heard the witch call out the same words.

On the fourth day, the prince returned in the afternoon. He waited until the witch had climbed back down Rapunzel's hair and disappeared. Then he stood under the window and called up: "Rapunzel, Rapunzel, let down your hair to me!"

At first Rapunzel was frightened. She did not recognize the voice calling up to her. When she looked out of the window, she saw the handsome prince below. The prince told her that he was a friend and Rapunzel agreed to let him up.

Rapunzel and the prince had a lovely time, talking and laughing. Rapunzel had never spoken to anyone except the witch before!

The prince returned to the tower often. Each time,
he waited until the witch had gone and then called
up to Rapunzel to let down her hair.

Day after day, the prince and Rapunzel talked and laughed. Very soon they had fallen in love! The prince told Rapunzel that he wanted to take her out of the tower and the two began to plan her escape.

Finally, the day came for the prince to free Rapunzel. But just as they were preparing to leave the tower, they heard a voice below....

"Rapunzel, Rapunzel, let down your hair to me," the witch
called from the ground.

"She must not find you here!" Rapunzel told the prince.
But there was nowhere for him to hide! Rapunzel had
no choice. She had to let the witch into the tower.

When the witch saw the prince she flew into a rage.
"You'll not visit my Rapunzel again," she shrieked.
She grabbed some scissors and cut off Rapunzel's hair.
"Now, go!" the witch shouted at the prince.
With a mighty shove, she pushed him out of the window.

"No, please!" cried Rapunzel as the prince fell. She ran to the window and leaned out so far that she tumbled out of the tower, too! Luckily, Rapunzel and the prince landed in some soft bushes and were not hurt. As they looked at each other the two started to laugh. Without Rapunzel's hair, the witch was the one stuck in the tower!

The prince helped Rapunzel to her feet. Then he gently led her to his horse and helped her climb on. He jumped on to his horse behind her and the two quickly rode off, leaving the witch behind for good.

The prince had discovered who Rapunzel's parents were. He took her to them. They had missed their daughter terribly all these years and were thrilled to have her back!

The prince left Rapunzel with her family –
they had a lot of catching up to do! But he
came by to visit her every day.

Not long after that, Rapunzel and the prince were married. There was great happiness throughout the land.

Rapunzel planted a beautiful garden near the castle, where she grew lots of the delicious lettuce after which she had been named.

The witch spent the rest of her life locked up in the tower. Rapunzel and her prince lived happily ever after.

The End